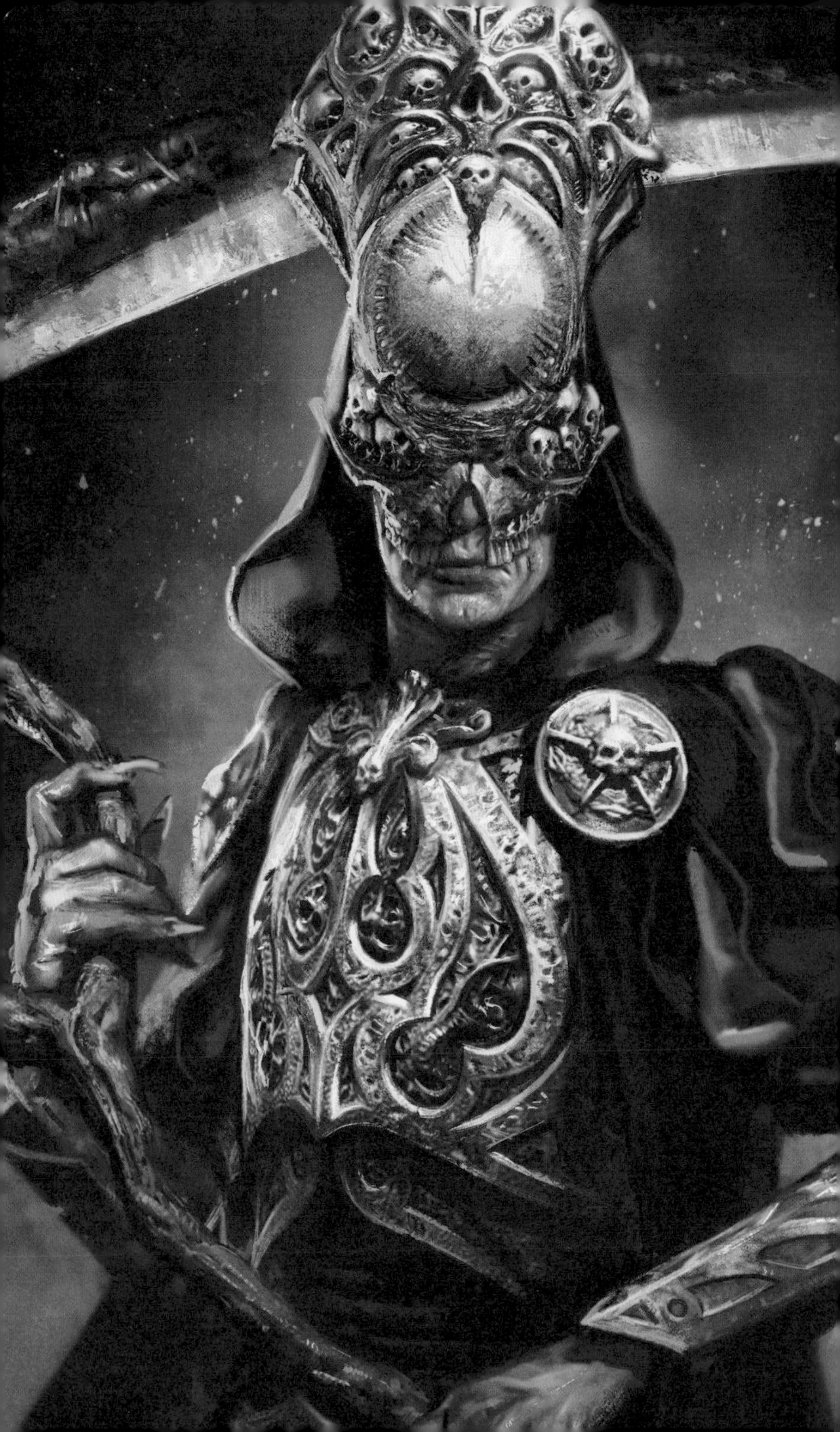

If I tell you about DEATH, will you tell me about LIFE?

Despite what you may think of me, I promise you there is existence beyond the Mortal Realm. You fear what you don't understand, and that is how I came to be known as Death, though I prefer to be called the Alltaker.

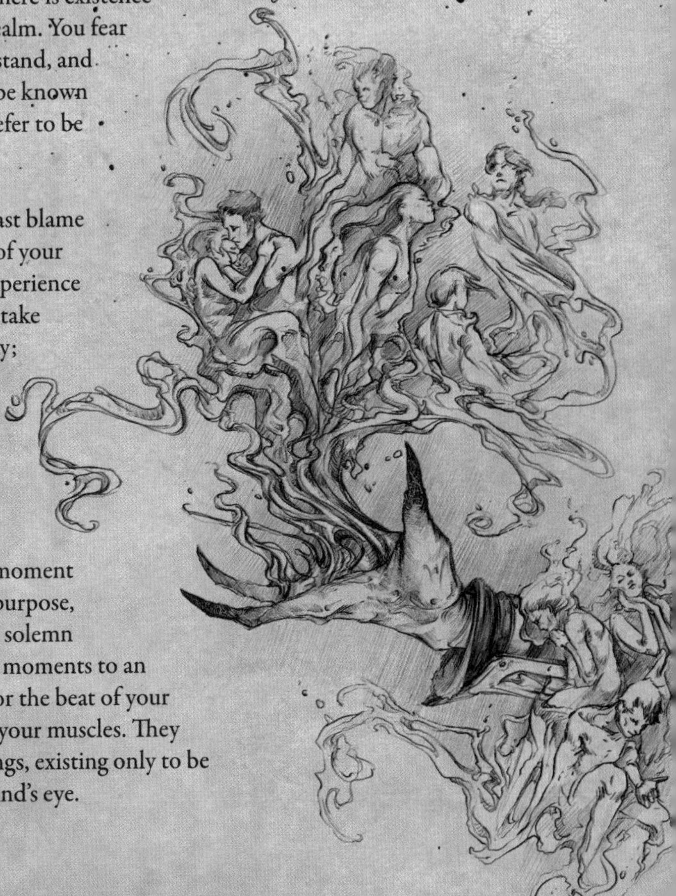

It is not my place to cast blame on the shortcomings of your senses. All that you experience is all that you know. I take those experiences away; a scary prospect, but not a malicious one. They are as special to me as they once were to you.

I have never found a moment lived that carried no purpose, though it remains my solemn duty to bring all such moments to an end. I have no need for the beat of your heart, or the pulse of your muscles. They are impermanent things, existing only to be embalmed in your mind's eye.

Memory.

It is all there is.

It is all you are now.

When you expire, the brilliance of your experience is sealed within all that you touch. The glass you drink from every morning can never be cleaned of the relief you feel as cool water touches your lips. The coin you fiddled with in your pocket as you first nervously spoke to the object of your desire has much greater value than the number stamped on its face. These memories are a great currency of their own in the next life.

Take up your pen, and inscribe the contents of your heart for those are what matter once it stops beating.

The pen you use to write your stories will long remember the relieving pressure of immortalizing on the page your inner monologue. So pick it up and do the easiest thing in the world...

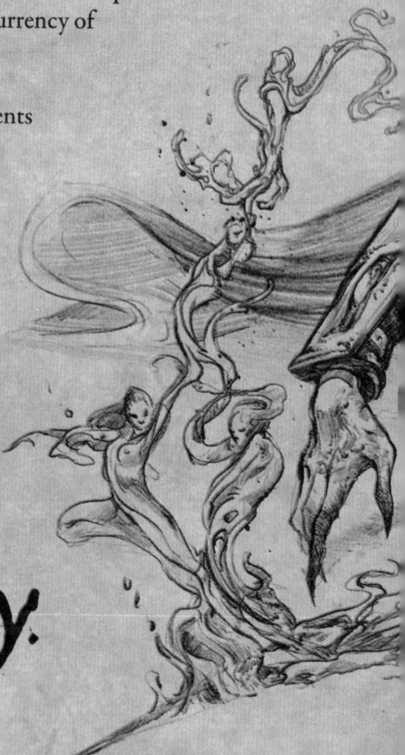

Tell me your story.

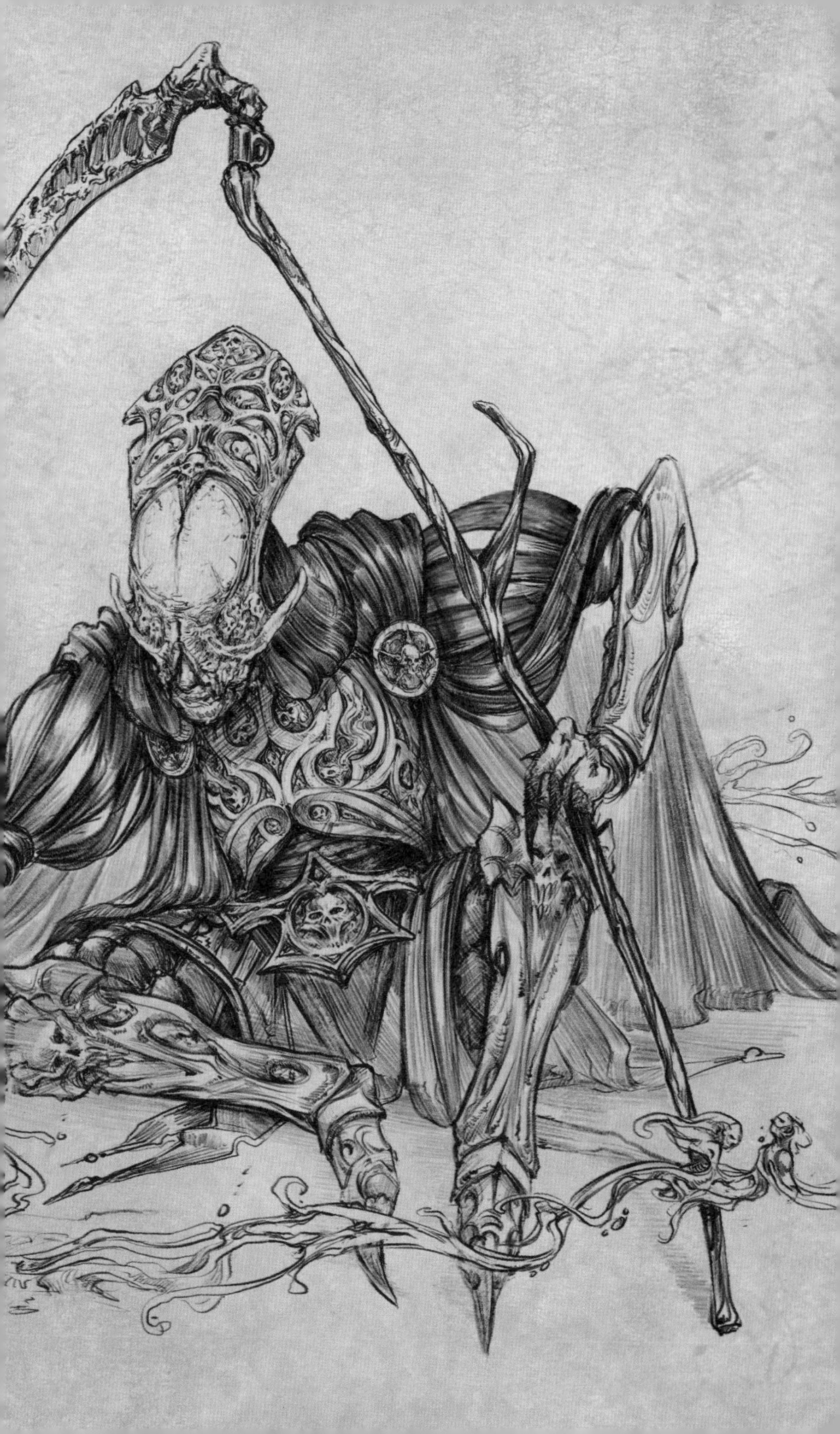

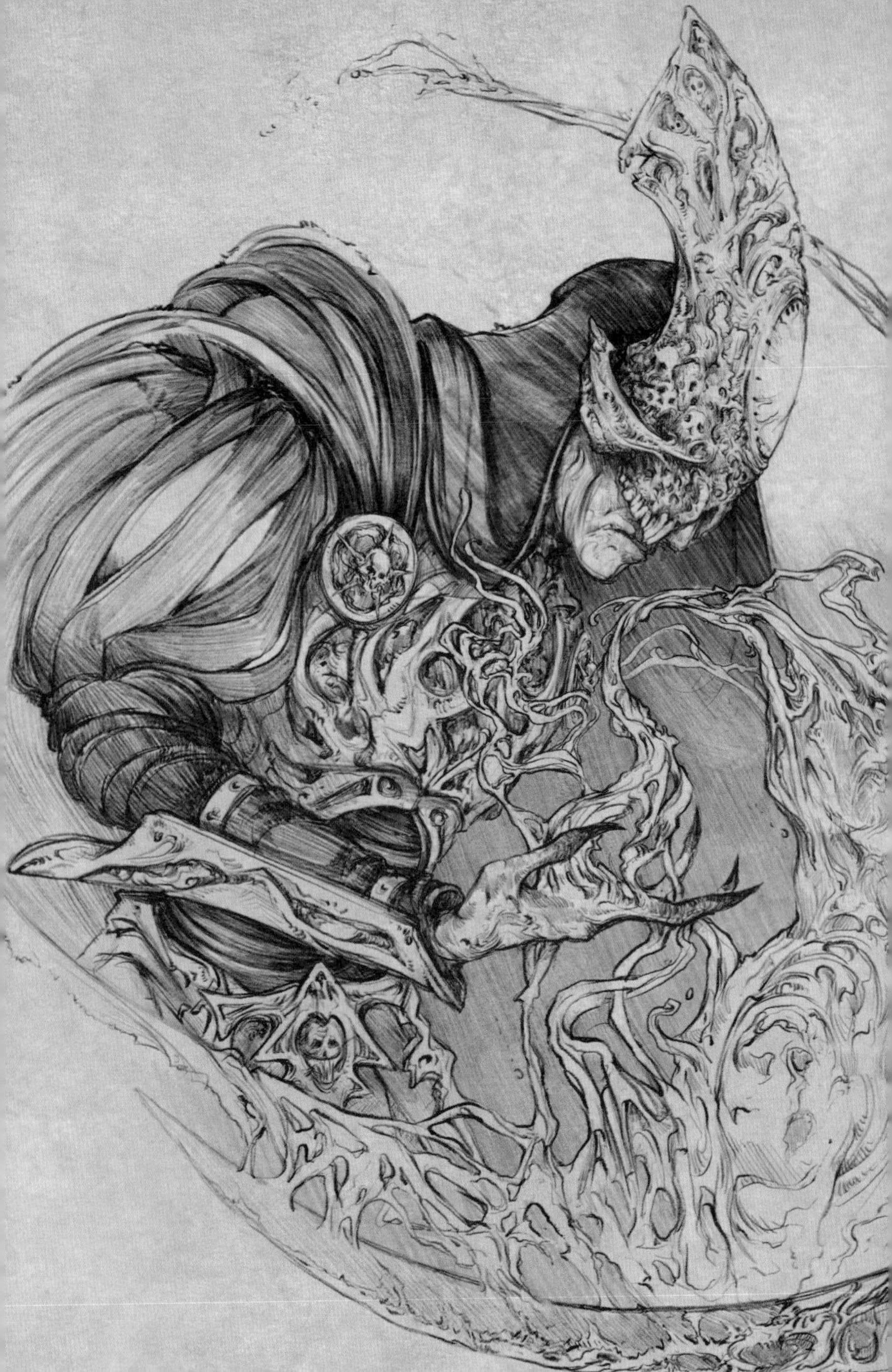

Let not the end of our journey be the end of our travels.

There are new memories to create, be they great or small, joyous or lamenting. Do not let them leave you, as ash from the funeral pyre trails off into the night sky. Do not keep them to yourself, as the corpse is consumed by the blaze. Share them. Be the inferno, raging against the horizon. Let all that you touch come to know your mark.

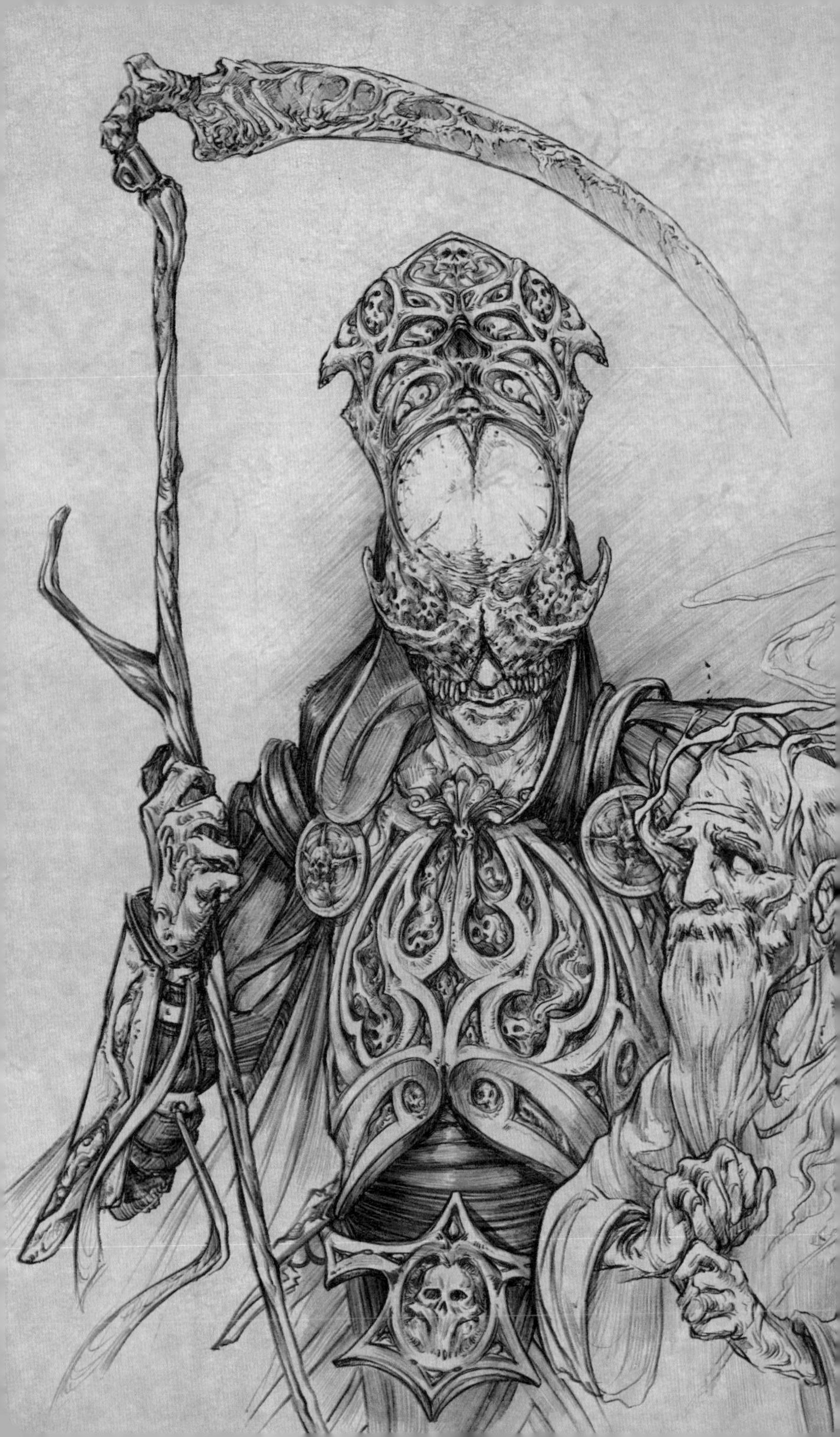

These pages are alive.
These pages are sacred.

I promise you, they will be alive long after you die. As I told you before, I come for everyone and yes, some day I will come for you.

So, you have come to and end here but I will grant that you have not come to

THE END.

Yet...

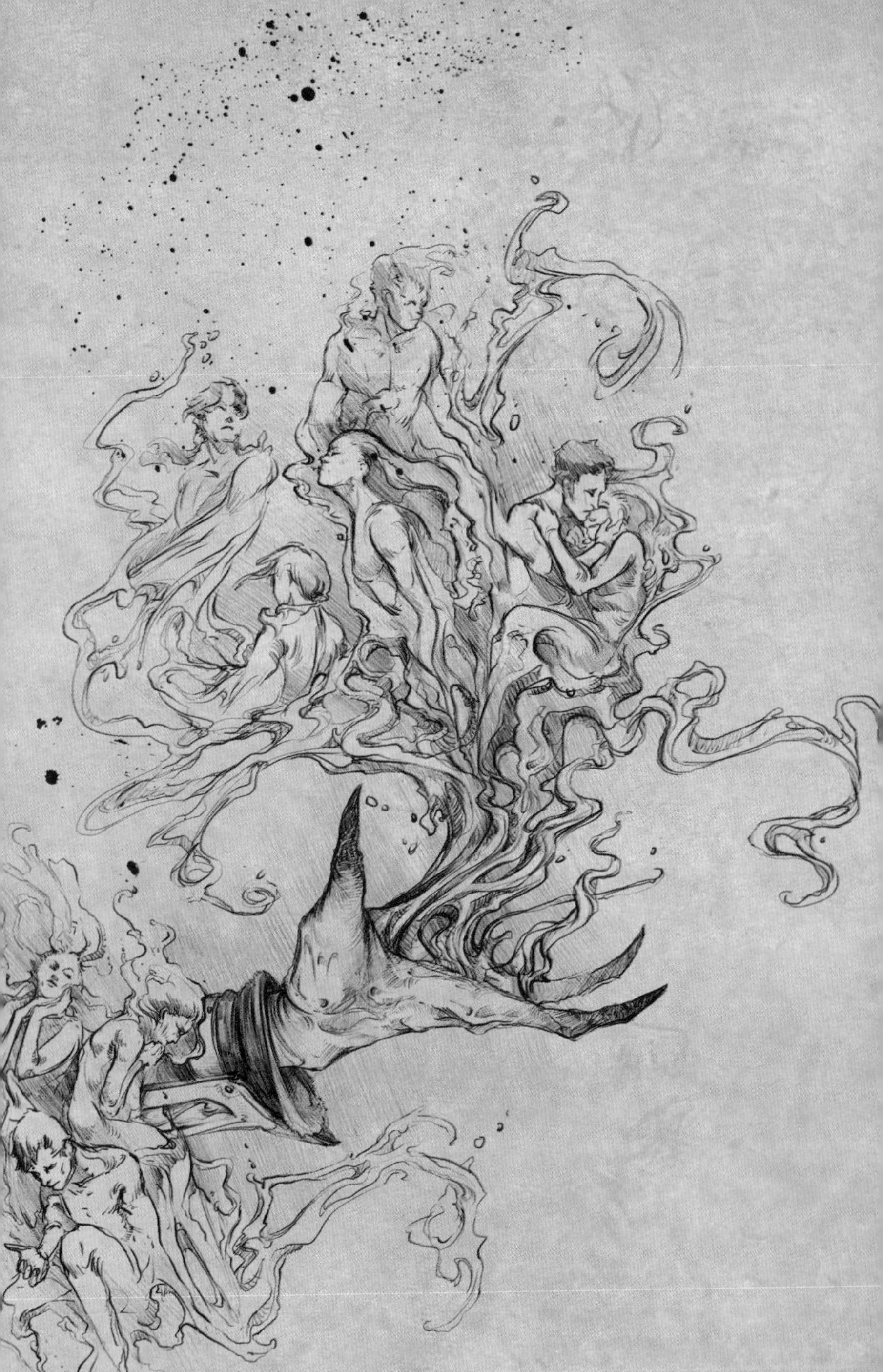

COURT OF THE DEAD.

is created by Tom Gilliland

Illustrations: Rachel Roubicek
Writer: Jacob Murray
Design: Ricky Lovas
Editor: Anna Van Slee

INSIGHTS

INSIGHT EDITIONS

San Rafael, California
www.insighteditions.com

MANUFACTURED IN CHINA

10 9 8 7 6 5 4 3 2 1